Anno's
PEEKABOO

Mitsumasa Anno

Philomel Books
New York

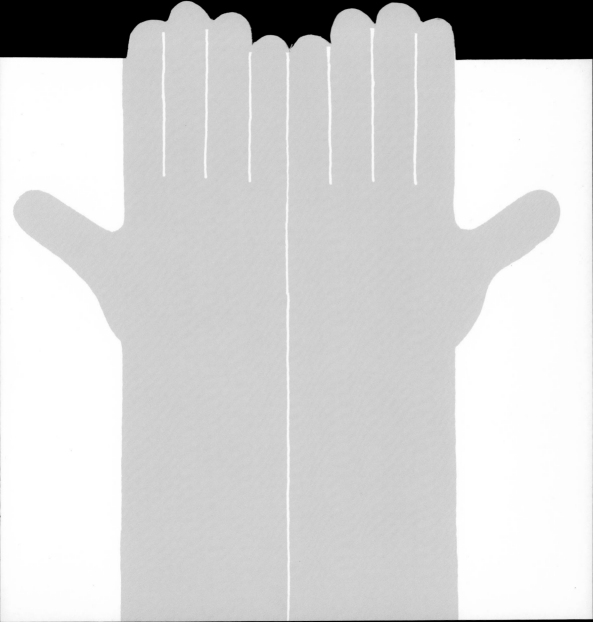

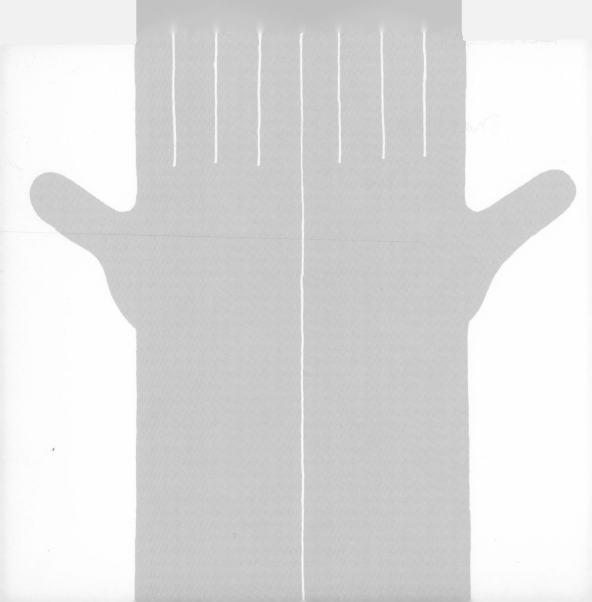

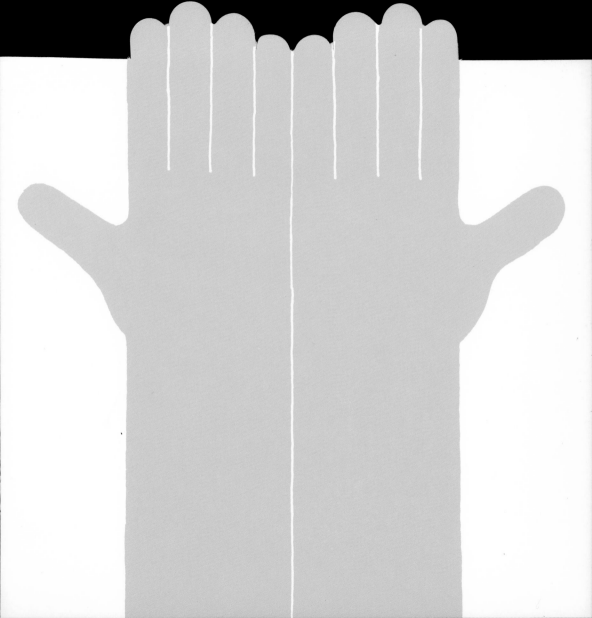

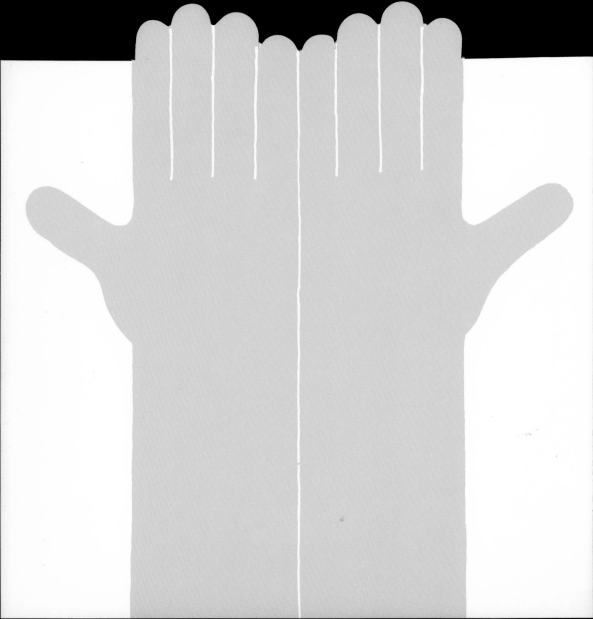

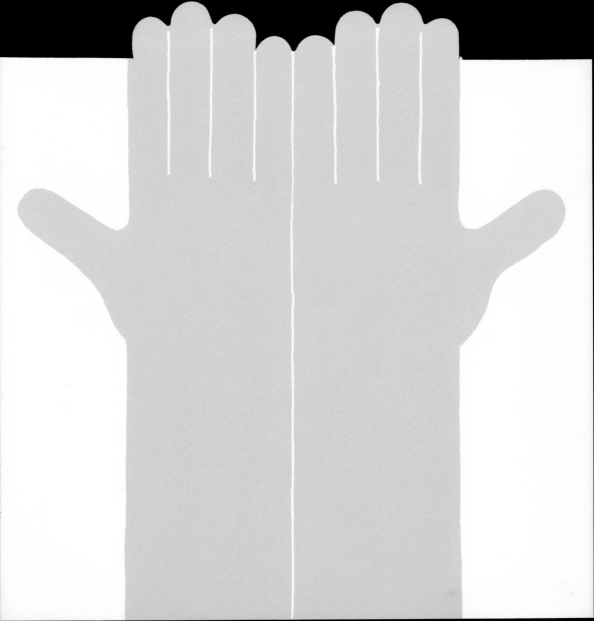

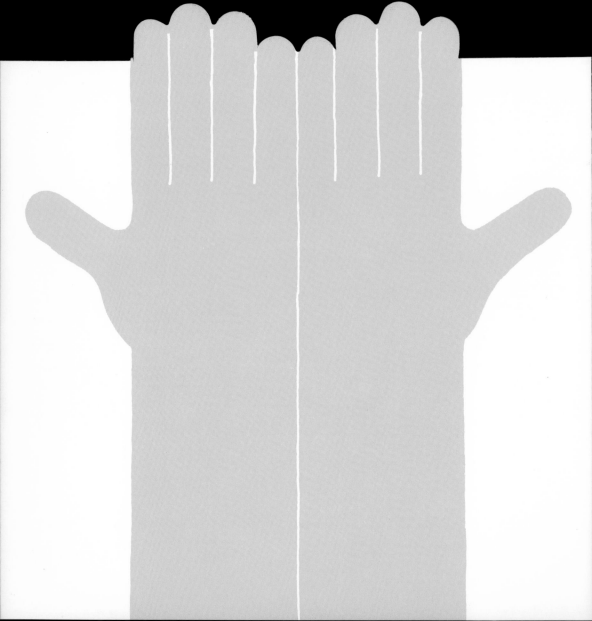

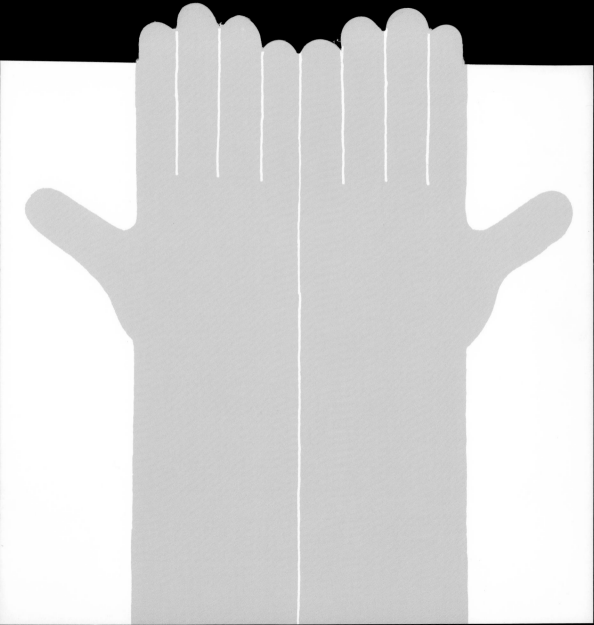

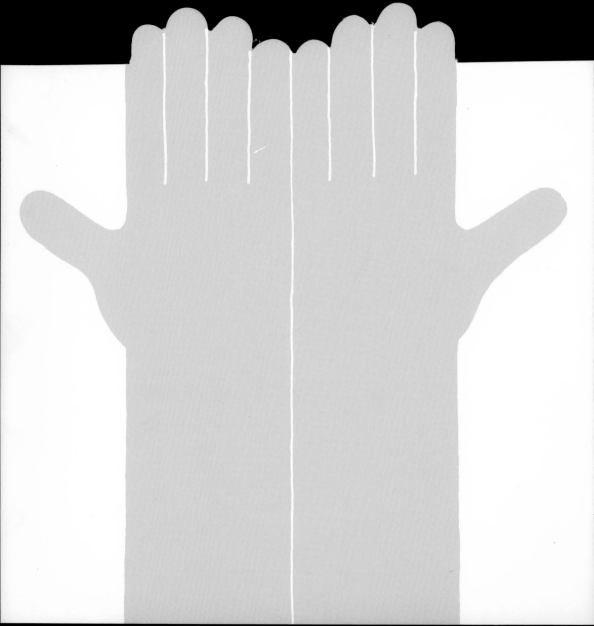

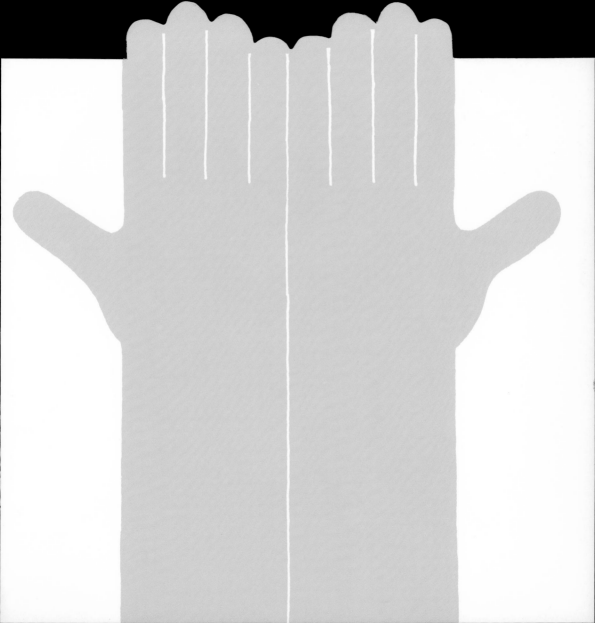

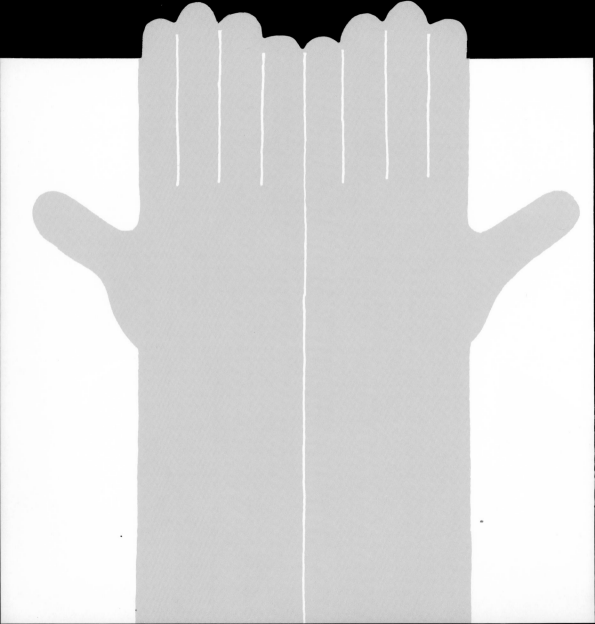

Mitsumasa Anno
is known the world over for his highly
original and thought-provoking picture books.
In 1984 he was awarded the Hans Christian Andersen Medal,
the highest honor attainable in the field of children's
book illustration. Born in 1926 in Western Japan,
Mr. Anno is a graduate of the Yamaguchi Teacher
Training College and worked for some time as a teacher
before becoming an artist. He has recently become
a grandfather and this is his first book
for very young children.

Copyright © 1987 by Kūso-Kōbō. All rights reserved.
Published by Philomel Books, a division of The Putnam & Grosset Group,
200 Madison Avenue, New York, NY 10016. Originally published by Dowaya Publishers,
Japan, under the title *Inai Inai Baa No Ehon*. American rights arranged with
Dowaya through Japan Foreign-Rights Centre, Japan. Printed in Singapore.
Library of Congress Cataloging-in-Publication Data
Anno, Mitsumasa, 1926 —   Anno's peekaboo.
Summary: The reader is invited to play a game of peekaboo with a variety of
animals and people. [1. Games — Fiction.   2. Animals — Fiction.   3. Stories
without words]   I. Title.   II. Title: Peekaboo. PZ7.A5875Arl   1988
[E]   87-7255   ISBN 0-399-21520-5   Third impression